$ THREE THOUSAND DOLLARS

Anna Katharine Green

Pharos Books

ISBN: 978-93-59838-89-2
eISBN: 978-93-59831-09-1

©Publisher

Publisher: Pharos Books (P) Ltd.
Plot No.-63, Main Mother Dairy Road
Pandav Nagar, East Delhi-110092
Phone: 011-40395855, +4049916623
WhatsApp: +91 8368220032
E-mail: sales@pharosbooks.in
Website: www.pharosbooks.in
First Edition: 2024

Printed By: Sushma Book Binding House, Okhla
Industrial Area, Phase II, New Delhi-110020

THREE THOUSAND DOLLARS
By Anna Katharine Green

CONTENTS

CHAPTER I

"Do you know what would happen to him?"

"NOW state your problem."

The man who was thus addressed shifted uneasily on the long bench which he and his companion bestrode. He was facing the speaker, and though very little light sifted through the cobweb-covered window high over their heads, he realized that what there was fell on his features, and he was not sure of his features, or of what effect their expression might have on the other man.

"Are you sure we are quite alone in this big, desolate place?" he asked.

It seemed a needless question. Though it was broad daylight outside and they were in the very heart of the most populated district of lower New York, they could not have been more isolated had the surrounding walls been those of some old ruin in the heart of an untraversed desert.

A short description of the place will explain this. They were in the forsaken old church not far from Avenue A———, a building long given over to desolation, and empty of everything but débris and one or two broken stalls, which for some inscrutable reason—possibly from some latent instinct of inherited reverence—had not yet been converted into junk and sold to the old clothes men by the rapacious denizens of the surrounding tenements.

Perhaps you remember this building; perhaps some echo of the bygone and romantic has come to you as you passed its decaying walls once dedicated to worship, but soulless now and only distinguishable from the five-story tenements pressing up on either side, by its one high window in which some bits of colored glass still lingered amid its twisted and battered network. You may remember the building and you may remember the stray glimpses afforded you through the arched opening in the lower story of one of the adjacent tenements, of the churchyard in its rear with its chipped and tumbling headstones just showing here and there above the accumulated litter. But it is not probable that you have any recollections of the interior of the church itself, shut as it has been from the eye of the public for nearly a generation. And it is with the interior we have to do—a great hollow vault where once altar and priest confronted a reverent congregation. There is no altar here now, nor any chancel; hardly any floor. The timbers which held the pews have rotted and fallen away, and what was once a cellar has received all this rubbish and held it piled up in mounds which have blocked up most of the windows and robbed the place even of the dim religious light which was once its glory, so that when the man whose words we have just quoted asked if they were quite alone and peered into the dim, belumbered corners, it was but natural for his hardy, resolute, and unscrupulous companion to snort with impatience and disgust as he answered:

"Would I have brought you here if I hadn't known it was the safest place in New York for this kind of talk? Why, man, there may be in this city five men all told, who know the trick of the door I unfastened for you, and not one of them is a cop. You may take my word for that. Besides—"

"But the kids? They're everywhere; and if one of them should have followed us—"

"Do you know what would happen to him? I'll tell you a story—no, I won't; you're frightened enough already. But there's no kid here, nor any one else but our two selves, unless it be some wandering spook from the congregations laid outside; and spooks don't count. So out with your proposition, Mr. Fellows. I—"

THREE THOUSAND DOLLARS

CHAPTER II

"Thousands in that safe"

"NO names!" hoarsely interrupted the other. "If you speak my name again I'll give the whole thing up."

"No you won't; you're too deep in it for that. But I'll drop the Fellows and just call you Sam. If that's too familiar, we'll drop the job. I'm not so keen on it."

"You will be. It's right in your line." Sam Fellows, as he was called, was whispering now—a hot, eager whisper, breathing of guilt and desperation. "If I could do it alone—but I haven't the wit—the———"

"Experience," dryly put in the other. "Well, well!" he exclaimed impatiently, as Fellows crept nearer, but said nothing.

"I'm going to speak, but—Well, then, here's how it is!" he suddenly conceded, warned by the other's eye. "The building is a twenty-story one, chuck full and alive with business. The room I mean is on the twelfth floor; it is one of five, all communicating, and all in constant use except the one holding the safe. And that is visited constantly. Some one is always going in and out. Indeed, it is a rule of the firm that every one of the employees must go into that room once, at least, during the day, and remain there for five minutes alone. I do it; every one does it; it's a very mysterious proceeding which only a crank like my employer would devise."

"What do you do there?"

"Nothing. I'm speaking now for myself. The others—some of the others—*one* of the others may open the safe. That's what I believe, that's what I want to know about and *how it's done*. There are thousands in that safe, and the old man being away—"

"Yes, this is all very interesting. Go on. What you want is an artist with a jimmy."

"No, no. It's no such job as that. I want to know the person, the trusted person who has all those securities within touch. It's a mania with me. I should have been the man. I'm—I'm *manager.*"

The hoarseness with which this word was uttered, the instinct of shame which made his eyes fall as it struggled from his lips, wakened a curious little gleam of hardy cynicism in the steady gaze of his listener.

"Oh, you're manager, are you!" came in slow retort, filling a silence that had more of pain than pleasure in it. "Well, manager, your story is very interesting, but by no means complete. Suppose you hurry on to the next instalment."

Cringing as from a blow, Fellows took up his tale, no longer creeping nearer his would-be confederate, but, if anything, edging away.

CHAPTER III

"How does it stand"

"I'VE watched and watched and watched," said he, "but I can't pick out the man. Letters come, orders are given, and those orders are carried out, but *not by me*. I'm speaking now of investments, or the payment of large sums; anything which calls for the opening of that safe where the old man has stuffed away his thousands. Small matters fall to my share. There is another safe, of which I hold the combination. Child's play, but the other! It would make both of us independent, and yet leave something for appearances. But it can't be worked. It stands in front of a glass door from which the curtain is drawn every night. Every passerby can look in. If it is opened it must be done in broad daylight and by the person whom the old man trusts. By that means only would I get my revenge, and revenge is what I want. He don't trust me, *me* who have been with him for seven years and—"

"Drop that, it isn't interesting. The facts are what I want. What kind of safe is it?"

"The strangest you ever saw. I don't know who made it. There's nothing on it to show. Nor is there a lock or combination. But it opens. You can just see the outline of a door. Steel—fine steel, and not so very large, but the contents—"

"We'll take its contents for granted. How does it stand? On a platform?"

"Yes, one foot from the floor. The platform runs all the way across the room and holds other things; a table which nobody uses, a revolving bookcase and a series of shelves, fitted with boxes containing old receipts and such junk. Sometimes I go through these; but nothing ever comes of it." He paused, as if the subject were distasteful.

"And the safe is opened?"

"Almost every week. I'm ashamed to tell you the old duffer's methods; they're loony. But he isn't a lunatic. At any rate, they don't think so in Wall Street."

"I'll make a guess at his name."

"Not yet. You'll have to swear——"

"Oh, we're both in it. Never mind the heroics. It's too good a thing to peach on. Me and the manager! I like that. Take it easy till the job's done, anyway. And now I'll take a fly at the name. It's——"

He had the grace to whisper.

CHAPTER IV

"Stenographers must be counted"

YOUNG Fellows squirmed and turned a shade paler, if one could trust the sickly violet ray that shot down from the once exquisitely colored window high up over their heads.

"Hush!" he muttered; and the other grinned. Evidently the guess was a correct one.

"No, he's no lunatic," the professional quietly declared. "But he has queer ways. Which of his queers do you object to?"

"When his letters come, or more often his cablegrams, they are opened by me and then put in plain view on a certain little bulletin board in the main office. These are his orders. Any one who knows the cipher can read them. I don't know the cipher. At night I take them down, number them, and file them away. They have served their purpose. They have been seen by the person whose business it is to carry out his instructions, and the rest you must guess. His brokers know the secret, but it is never discussed by us. The least word and the next cablegram would read in good plain English, 'Fire him!' I've had that experience. I've had to fire three since he went away two months ago."

"That's good."

"Why good?"

"That cuts out three from your list. The person is not among the ones dismissed."

"That's so." New life seemed to spring up in Fellows. "You'll do the job," he cried. "Somehow, I never thought of going about it that way. And I know another man that's out."

"Who?"

"Myself, for one. There are only seven more."

"Counting all?"

"All."

"Stenographers included?"

"Oh, stenographers!"

"Stenographers must be counted."

"Well, then, seven men and one woman. Our stenographer is a woman."

"What kind of a woman?"

"A young girl. Ordinary, but good enough. I've never noticed her very much."

"Tell me about the men."

"What's the use? You wouldn't take my word. They're a cheap lot, beneath contempt in my estimation. There's not one of them clever enough for the business. Jack Forbush comes the nearest to it, and probably is the one. The way he keeps his eye on me makes me suspect him. Or is he, too, playing my game?"

"How can I tell? How can I tell anything from what you say? I'll have to look into the matter myself. Give me the names and addresses and I'll look the parties up. Get their rating, so to speak. Leave it to me, and I'll land the old man's confidential clerk."

"Here's the list. I thought you might want it."

"Where's the girl's name?"

"The girl! Oh, pshaw!"

"Put her name down just the same."

"There, then. Grace Lee. Address, 74 East —— Street. And now swear on the honor of a gentleman——"

Beau Johnson pulled the rim of Fellows's hat over his eyes to suggest what he thought of this demand.

                    THREE THOUSAND DOLLARS

CHAPTER V

"I've business with him"

NEXT day there appeared at the offices of Thomas Stoughton, in Nassau Street, a trim, well-looking man, who had urgent business with Mr. Fellows, the manager. He was kept waiting for some time before being introduced into that gentleman's private room; but this did not seem to disturb him. There was plenty to look at, or so he seemed to think, and his keen, noncommittal eyes flashed hither and thither and from face to face with restless activity. He seemed particularly interested in the bookkeeper of the establishment, but it was an interest which did not last long, and when a neat, pleasant-faced young woman rose from her seat and passed rapidly across the room, it was upon her his eyes settled and remained fixed, with a growing attention, until a certain door closed upon her with a sound like a snapping lock. Then he transferred his attention to the door, and was still gazing at it when a boy summoned him to the manager's office.

He went in with reluctance. He had rather have watched that door. But he had questions to ask, and so made a virtue of necessity. Mr. Fellows was not pleased to see him. He started quite guiltily from his seat and only sat again on compulsion—the compulsion of his visitor's steady and quelling eye.

"I've business with you, Mr. Fellows." Then, the boy being gone, "Which is the room? The one opening out of the general office directly opposite this?"

"He transferred his attention to the door"

Mr. Fellows nodded.

"I have just seen one of the employees go in there. I should like to see that person come out. Do you mind talking with this door open? I know enough about banking to hold up my end of the conversation."

Fellows rose with a jerk and pushed the door back. His visitor smiled easily and launched into a discussion about stocks and bonds interspersed with a few assertions and questions not meant for the general ear, as:

'It's the girl who is in there. Not ordinary, by any means. Just the sort an old smudge like Stoughton would be apt to trust. Now what's that?"

'Singing. She often sings. I've forbidden it, but she forgets, she says," *answered Fellows.*

'Pretty good music. Listen to that note. High as a prima donna's. Does she sing at her work?"

'No; I'd fire her if she did. It's only when she's walking about or when—"

'She's in that room?"

"Yes."

"At par? I buy nothing at par. There! She's coming. I wish I dared intercept her, rifle her pockets. Do you know if she has pockets?"

'No; how should I?"

'Fellows, you're not worth your salt. Ah! there's a face for you, and I can read it like a book. Did a letter or cablegram come to-day?"

'Yes; didn't you see it? Hung up in the outer office."

"I thought I saw something. Ninety-five? That's a quotation worth listening to. Three at ninety-five. *That girl's a trump. I will see more of my lady."* Here he took care to shut the door. "I've been the rounds, Fellows. Private-detective work and all that. She is the only puzzler among the group. You'll hear from me again; meanwhile treat the girl well. Don't spring any traps; leave that to me."

And Fellows, panting with excitement, promised, muttering under his breath:

"A woman! That's even worse than I thought. But we'll make the old fellow pay for it. Those securities are ours. I already feel them in my hand."

The sinister twitch which marred the other's mouth emphasized the assertion in a way Grace Lee's friends would have trembled to see.

CHAPTER VI

"If I could tell you his story"

THAT evening a young woman and a young man sat on one of the benches in Central Park. They were holding hands, but modestly and with a clinging affection. No one appeared in sight; they had the moon-light, the fragrance of the spring foliage, and their true love all to themselves. The woman was Grace, the young man was Philip Andrews, a candid-eyed, whole-hearted fellow whom any girl might be proud to be seen with, much more to be engaged to. Grace was proud, but she was more than that; her heart was all involved in her hope—a good heart which he was equally proud to have won. Yet while love was theirs and the surroundings breathed peace and joy, they did not look quite happy. A cloud was on his brow and something like a tear in her eye as she spoke gently but with rare firmness.

"Philip, we must wait. One love does not put out another. I cannot leave my old father now. He is too feeble and much too dependent on me. Philip, you do not know my father. You have seen him, it is true, many, many times. You have talked with him and even have nursed him at odd moments, when I had to be out of the room getting supper or supplying some of his many wants. Yet you do not know him."

"I know that he is intelligent."

"Yes, yes, that is evident. Any one can see that. And you can see, too, that he is frequently fretful and exacting, as all old people are. But the qualities he shows me—his strong, melancholy, but devoted nature, quickened by an unusually unhappy life—that you do not see and cannot, much as you like him and much as he likes you. Only the child who has surprised him at odd moments, when he thought himself quite alone, wringing his hands and weeping over some intolerable memory—who has listened in the dead of night to his smothered but heart-breaking groans, can know either his suffering or the one joy which palliates it. If I could tell you his story—but that would be treason to one whose rights I am bound to reverence. You will respect my silence, but you must also take my word that he needs and has a right to all the pleasure and all the hope my love can give him. I cannot be with him much; my work forbids, but the little time I have is his, except on rare occasions like this, and he knows it and is satisfied. Were I married———. But you will wait, Philip. It may not be long—he grows weaker every day. Besides, you are not ready yet yourself. You are doing wonderfully well, but a year's freedom will help you materially, as it will me. Every day is adding to our store; in a year we may be almost independent."

"Grace, you have misunderstood me. I said that I was no good without you, that I needed your presence to make a man of me, but I did not mean that you were to share my fortunes now. I would not ask that. I would be a fool or worse, for, Grace, I'm not doing so well as you think. While I knew that my present employment was for a specified time, I had hopes of continuing on. But this cannot be. That's what I have to tell you to-night. It looks as if our marriage would have to be postponed indefinitely instead of hastened. And I can't bear it. You don't know what you are to me, or what this disappointment is. I expected to be raised, not dismissed, and if I had had———"

"Grace, you have misunderstood me"

"What?"

The word came very softly, and with rare tenderness. It made him turn and look at her sweet, upturned face, with its resources of strength and shy, unfathomable smile. "What?" she asked again, with a closer pressure of her hand. "You must finish all your sentences with *me*."

"I'm ashamed." He uttered it breathlessly. "What am I, to say, 'If I had three thousand dollars the Stickney Company would keep me?' I have barely three hundred and those are dedicated to you."

CHAPTER VII

"I'm sure that I can get them for you"

"IF you had *three thousand*!" She repeated it in surprise and yet with an indescribable air, which to one versed in human nature would have caught the attention and aroused strange inner inquiries. "Does the Stickney Company want money so badly as that?"

"That's not it. They have plainly told me that for three thousand dollars and my services they would give me ten thousand dollars' stock interest, but insist that the man who assumes the responsibility of the position must be financially interested as well. But I haven't the money, and without the money my experience appears to them valueless. I despair of getting another situation in these hard times and—Grace, you don't look sorry."

"Because—" she paused, and her fine eyes roamed about her jealous of a listener to her secret, but did not pierce the bush which rose up, cloudy with blossoms, a few feet behind their bench—"because it is not impossible for you to hope for those thousands. I think—I am sure that I can get them for you."

Her voice had sunk to a whisper, but it was a very clear whisper.

Young Andrews looked at her in surprise; there was something besides pleasure in that surprise.

"Where?" he asked.

She hesitated, and just at that moment the moon slipped behind a cloud.

"Where, Grace, can you get three thousand dollars? From Mr. Stoughton? He is generous to you, he pays you well for what you do for him, but I do not think he would give you that amount, nor do I think he would risk it on any venture involving my judgment. I should not like to have you ask him. I should like to rise feeling absolutely independent of Mr. Stoughton."

"I never thought of asking him. There is another way. I'd—I'd like to think it over. If your scheme is good—*very* good, I might be brought to aid you in the way my mind suggests. But I should want to be sure."

She was not looking at him now. If she had been, she might have been startled at his expression. Nor could he see her face; she had turned it aside.

"Grace," he prayed, "don't do anything rash. You handle so much money that three thousand dollars may seem very little to you. But it's a goodly sum to get or to replace if one loses it. You must not borrow—"

"I will not borrow."

"Nor raise it in any way without telling me the sacrifice you must make to obtain it. But it's all a dream; tell me that it's all a dream; you were talking from your wishes, not from any certainty you have. Say so, and I will not be disappointed. I do not want *your* money; I'd rather go poor and wait till the times change. Don't you see? I'd be more of a man."

"But you'd have to take it if I gave it to you, and—perhaps I shall. I want to see you happy, Philip; I must see you happy. I'd be willing to risk a good deal for that. I'm not so happy myself, father suffers so, and the care of it weighs on me. You are all I have to make me glad, and when you are troubled my heart goes down, down. But it's getting late, dear. It's time we went home. Don't ask me what's in my mind, but dream of riches. I'm sure they will come. You shall earn them with the three thousand dollars you want and which I will give you."

"I shall earn them honestly," were the last words he said, as they rose from the seat and began to move toward the gate. And the moon, coming out from its temporary eclipse, shone on his clear-cut face as he said this, but not on her bowed head and sidelong look. They were in the shadow.

There was something else in the shadow. As they moved away and disappeared in the darkness the long, slim figure of a man rose from behind the bush I have mentioned. He had a sparkling eye and a thin-lipped mouth, and he smiled very curiously as he looked after the pair before turning himself about and going the other way.

It was not Fellows; it was his chosen confederate in the nefarious scheme they had planned between them.

CHAPTER VIII

"I did as you bid me"

A NOTHER meeting in the old church, but this time at night. The somberness of the surroundings was undiminished by any light. They were in absolute darkness. Absolute darkness, but not absolute silence. Noises strange and suggestive, but not of any human agency, whispered, sighed, rattled, and grumbled from far away recesses. The snap of wood, the gnawing of rats, the rustling of bat wings disturbed the ears of one of the guilty pair, till his voice took on unnatural tones as he tried to tell his story to his greedy companion. They were again astride the bench, and their thin faces were so near that their breaths commingled at times; yet Fellows felt at moments so doubtful of all human presence that instinctively his hand would go groping out till it touched the other's arm or breast, when it would fall back again satisfied. He was in a state of absolute terror of the darkness, the oppressive air, the ghostly sounds, and possibly of the image raised by his own conscience, yet he hugged to himself the thought of secrecy which it all involved, and never thought of yielding up his scheme or even shortening his tale, so long as the other listened and gave his mind to the problem which promised them thousands without the usual humdrum method of working for them.

We will listen to what he had to say, leaving to your imagination the breaks and guilty starts and moments of intense listening and anxious fear with which he seasoned it.

"I did as you bid me," he whispered. "Yesterday fresh orders came from abroad, in cipher, as usual. (It's an unreadable cipher. I've had experts on it many times.) I had hung it up, and though business was heavy, my business, you know, I had eyes for our fair friend, and knew every step she took about the offices. I even knew when her eyes first fell on the cablegram. I had my door open, and I caught her looking up from her work, and what was more, caught the pause in the click-click of the typewriter as she looked and read. If she had not been able to read, the click-click would have gone on, for I believe she could work that typewriter with her eyes shut. But her attention was caught, and she stopped. I tell you I've been humiliated for the last time. I'm in for anything that will make that girl step down and out. What was that!"

Muttered curses from his companion brought him back to his story. With a gulp he went on:

"You may bet your bottom dollar that I watched her after that, and sure enough, in less than half an hour she had gone into the room where the safe is. Instantly I prepared my *coup d'état*. I waited just long enough to hear her voice in that one song she sings, then I jumped from my seat and rushed to the door, shouting, 'Miss Lee! Miss Lee! Your father! Your father!' making hullabaloo enough to raise the dead and scare her out of her wits; for she dotes on that old man and would sell her soul for his sake, I do believe.

"Great heavens, it worked! As I live, it worked. I heard her voice fail on that high upper note of hers, and then the sound of her feet staggering, slipping over the floor, and in another moment the fumbling of her hand on the knob and the slow opening of the door which she seemed to have no power to manage. Helping her, I pulled it open, and there beyond her and her white, shocked face, I saw—I saw———"

CHAPTER IX

"'The safe door is opened,' I cried"

"GO on! Don't be a fool; that was nothing."

"I don't know; it was like a great sigh at my ear. But this is awful! Couldn't we have one spark of light?"

"And have the police upon us the next minute? Look up at that window. You can see it, can't you?"

"Yes, yes, but very faintly," Fellows whispered.

"But you can see it. So could those outside, if we had one glimmer of light in here. No, no, you'll have to stand the dark or quit. But you shan't quit till you've told me what you saw in the room where the safe is."

"The safe door opening." His voice trembled so that the other shook him to steady his nerves. "Not opened, mind you, but opening. It was like magic, and I stared so that she forgot her fears and forgot her questions. Turning from me with a startled cry, she looked behind her, and saw what I saw, and tried to push me out. 'I'll come, I'll come,' she whispered. 'Leave me a minute and I'll come.'

"But I wasn't going to do that. 'The safe door is opened,' I cried. 'Did you do it?' She didn't know what to say. I have never seen a woman in such a state; then she whispered in awful agitation, 'Yes; I've been given the combination by Mr. Stoughton. I'm duly following his orders. But my father! What about my father? You frightened me so I forgot that—' I waited, staring at her, but she didn't finish. She just asked, 'My father? What has happened to him?' 'Nothing serious,' I managed to say. I wished the old father was in ballyhack. But he'd served his turn; I must say that he'd served his turn. 'A telephone message,' I went on.

'He had had a nervous spell and wanted you. I said that you could go home at noon.' She stood looking at me doubtfully; then her eyes stole back to the safe. 'You will have to leave me here for a few minutes,' she said. 'I have Mr. Stoughton's business to attend to. He will not be pleased at my having given away his secret. He did not wish it known who controlled his affairs in his absence, but now that you do know, you will be doing the right thing to let me go on in the way he has planned for me. His orders must be carried out.'

"She is very determined, and understands herself only too well, but I am manager, and I paid her back in her own coin. 'That's all very well,' said I, 'but what proof have I that you are telling me the truth? You have opened the safe—you say you have the combination— but people sometimes surprise a combination and open a safe from other interests than those of their employer. You seem a good girl, but *you are a girl,* and there are men here much more likely to be in Mr. Stoughton's confidence than yourself. With that open safe before us I cannot leave you here alone. What you take from it I must see, and if possible be present at your negotiations. That I consider a manager's duty under the circumstances.' 'Mr. Fellows,' she asked, 'can you read this morning's telegram?' 'No,' I felt bound to reply. 'Then that acquits you. I can.' And again she tried to urge me to go out. But I would not be urged. I was staring across the room at the open safe and in fancy clutching its contents. In fact, I made one step toward them. But she drew herself up with such an air that I paused. She's a big girl, you know, and not to be fooled with when she's angry. 'Come a step farther and I will scream for the watchman,' she whispered. All our talk had been low, for there were listening ears everywhere—we couldn't risk that, and I stepped back. Immediately she saw her advantage, and added, 'If you do not think better of it and leave the room, I'll scream.' For answer to this I said that I—"

CHAPTER X

"I have a scheme"

"WHAT?"

A yell answered him.

"Something hit me! Something hit me!"

"Yes, I hit you; and I'll hit you again if you don't go on."

Fellows shivered, attempted some puerile protest, balked, and stammeringly obeyed his restless and irritated companion.

"I—I said—I wasn't such a fool then as I am now—that she had lied when she told me that she had the combination. There was no combination. The safe did not even have a lock. The door opened with a spring. How had she induced that spring to give way? I demanded to know."

"And did she tell you?"

"No. She merely repeated, 'I will scream, and that will cause a scandal which will lead to your discharge, not mine.' So—so, I came out."

"Blast your eyes! And when did *she* come out?"

"Within five minutes. I watched the clock."

"And what did she have?"

"Nothing in sight."

"I see. A deep game. But I know a deeper. There is no possibility of breaking into that safe by night, undetected by the watchman?"

"None; and that watchman is incorruptible. The whole contents of the safe wouldn't move him to connect himself with this job."

"The job must be done by day and during office hours?"

"Yes."

"And cannot be done without the assistance of this girl?"

"You've heard."

"Very well; I have a scheme. Now listen to me."

Not even the rat which at that minute nibbled at Fellows's boot heel could have heard what followed. The panting of two breasts was, however, audible; and when, fifty minutes later, both crawled out of the cellar window among the rubbish which littered the rear of this once holy place, the one was trembling with excitement and the other with fear. They parted at the first thoroughfare, neither having eyes to see nor hearts to appreciate the touching scene which miles away was taking place in a little flat not very far from Harlem. An old man, frail in body, but with a sturdy spirit yet, was looking up from his pillow at the loving face of a young girl who was bending over him.

"I cannot sleep to-night," he said to her; "I cannot sleep; but that must not disturb you. I have so many things to think, pleasant things; but you have only cares, and must rest from them. You look very tired to-night, tired and worried. Leave me and sleep. I want to see you bright in the morning."

"An old man was looking up at the loving face of a young girl"

CHAPTER XI

"She will go in"

"THE next day there was a dearth of assistants in the office. One was sick, one had pleaded a long-delayed vacation, two had business for the concern which took them into different quarters of the city, and Mr. Beers, who was next in authority to Mr. Fellows, had been summoned to serve on the grand jury. Perhaps it was this knowledge that Mr. Beers would be absent which had led to the manager's easiness in regard to the others. For he had been easy, or so Miss Lee thought when she arrived in the morning and saw the office almost empty. However, it did not trouble her much. On the contrary, the quiet and non-surveillance of the two clerks who did the business of the day seemed rather to elate her, and she went about her work, copying letters and taking down notes with an alacrity and air of cheerful hope which caused the manager to cast toward her more than one suspicious look from his desk in the adjoining room. *He* was not busy, though he had been the first to arrive that morning; and he had brought with him a large square package which he had taken into the room which held the safe. He pretended to be busy, but any one watching him closely would have noticed that his eyes, and not his hands, were all that were engaged, and they were anywhere but on his desk or the letter he appeared to be reading. An observer would also have noticed that his nervousness was of the extreme sort, and that the trembling which shook his whole body increased visibly whenever his glance fell on the door of Mr. Beers's private room, opening at his back. No one was supposed to be in that room to-day, and had Miss Lee not been one minute late this especial morning, perhaps there might not have been. But in that one minute's grace a man had entered the office who had not gone out again, and where could he be if not in that one closed room?

The room which held the safe was open as usual, and many of Mr. Fellows's glances traveled that way. He had entered it once only since his first hurried visit of the early morning, but only to pull down the shade over the glass in the door communicating with the outside hall. This was his usual custom, and it attracted no attention. Why shouldn't he enter it again? He thought he would. A fascination was upon him. The problem he had given Beau Johnson to solve was to receive a test this day which would make him a rich man or a felon; but before that hour why not make his own study, his own investigation? True, he had made these many times before, but not with such lights to guide him. He might learn—

But no, the very conceit was folly. He knew his own limitations, else he had not called in the services of this crook. He could learn nothing by himself, but he might look the place over and see if all was in shape for the great attempt. That was only his duty. Beau Johnson had a right to expect that of him. If the scrub woman had moved anything——

At the thought that this possibly might have happened, he jumped to his feet and hurried into the outer office; but when he turned toward the room of the safe, he met Miss Lee's eye fixed upon him with such a keen, inquiring look that he faltered in his determination, and went in another direction instead. *She* knew that he had no business in that room, and she also knew that he knew she knew this. Any pretense that he had would only rouse her suspicions, and these must be lulled to the point of security, or she might not enter there herself, and on her entering there everything depended. Almost immediately upon the thought he was back in his seat, and the weary moments crept on. Would she never make her accustomed visit to that room? No cablegram had come that morning, but she would find some reason for going in. Of that he had been assured by Johnson. Why, he had not been told. "She will go in," Beau Johnson had said, and Fellows believed him. He believed everything the other said, otherwise he could not have gone on with this business. But she was very long about it. Harlowe would be coming back—

CHAPTER XII

"A block of steel"

"AH, he had an idea! It was not his own, but for the moment he thought it was. He would leave the office himself and thus give her an opportunity to quit her work and shut herself up with the safe. But—(was his mind leaving him?) there was something to be done first. The way must be cleared for the man in hiding to enter that room before she did. How was this to be accomplished? A dozen suggestions had been given him by his confederate, but he had forgotten them all. He was in too great a whirl to think, yet he must think; some way must be found. Ah, he had it. Taking up the receiver at his side, he telephoned to a German friend to call him up in five minutes, giving him the number of the telephone in the farthest room. This he did in German, telling him it was a joke and that he was not to insist upon an answer. Then he waited. In five minutes this farther bell rang. Calling to Miss Lee, he asked her to answer for him, saying he was very busy. As she rose, he gave a preconcerted signal on the door of Mr. Beers's room. As she disappeared in the one beyond, the dapper figure of Johnson crossed the outer office and slipped into the one holding the safe. A minute later she was back reporting the message and getting instructions, but the one thing she had to fear had been done; the trap had been laid, and now for its victim!

It was not long before that victim responded to the call. On the departure of the manager from the room Grace Lee rose, and with a conscious look toward the two clerks, slipped across the floor to the open door of the safe room. Entering, she swung to the door, which closed with a snap; then, with just a moment of hesitation, in which she seemed to be trying to regain her breath, she passed quickly across to the safe and took up her stand before it. So directly and so quickly had she done this that she had not seen the slim, immovable figure drawn up against the wall at her right behind the projection of a large bookcase. Nor did any influence for good or evil cause her to turn after she had reached the safe. All her thoughts, all her hopes, all the dreams which she had cherished seemed to be concentrated in the blank, eyeless object which confronted her, impenetrable to all appearance—a block of steel without visible opening—an enigma among safes—the problem of all problems to every cracksman in town but one—which was about to be solved if one could judge from the thrill which now shook her, and in shaking her communicated the same excitement to the silent, breathless, determined man in her rear, watching her as the tiger watches the quarry, and with the same tiger spring latent in his eye. In a moment her secret would be out, and then—

 THREE THOUSAND DOLLARS

CHAPTER XIII

"I am from headquarters"

FOR just a minute Grace Lee paused before the blank door of the safe, then she passed around to an unused speaking tube in the neighboring wall. Halting before it, in low but distinct tones she began to sing the famous aria from "The Magic Flute."

All agog, with eyes starting and ears alert, the man behind listened and watched. Nothing happened.

Then came a change. Gradually her voice rose, sweet and piercing, till it reached that famous F in alt so rarely attempted, so exciting to the ear when fairly taken and fairly held. Grace Lee could take it, and as it hung, sweet and deliciously thrilling in the air, Beau Johnson saw, to his amazement, though he was in a way prepared for it, the heavy safe door slip softly ajar. She had done it with her voice. How, he could only vaguely guess. He was better educated than most of his class, or he could not have understood it at all. As it was, he laid it to the vibration caused by a certain definite note acting on some delicate mechanism set in accord with that note, which mechanism starting another and a stronger one gradually led up to that which drew the bolts and set the door ajar. Whether his theory were true or not mattered little at the moment. The event for which he waited had been accomplished and accomplished before his eyes. To profit by it was his next thought, and to this end he held himself ready for the spring which had laid latent in his eyes since he first saw her advance toward the safe.

She was ignorant of his presence. This was evident from the jaunty way she turned from the tube, still singing, but in a desultory way, which showed that her thoughts were no longer on her music. But she was not so engrossed that she did not see him. The moment that her face turned his way, her eyes enlarged, her body stiffened, her whole personality took on power and purpose and *she* sprang more quickly than he did and shut the safe door with one quick movement of her hand that fastened it as securely as before. Then she drew herself up to meet his rush, a noble figure of resolute womanhood which any other man would have hesitated to assail. But he was proof to any appeal of this kind. She had been quicker than he who was esteemed the readiest in his class, and he owed her a grudge, if only for that. Smiling—it was a way of his when deeply moved or deeply dangerous—he accosted her with smooth and treacherous words.

"Don't scream, young lady; screaming will do you no good. Mr. Fellows has left the business to me and I am quite competent to manage it. I am from headquarters—a detective. Yesterday you aroused the manager's suspicions, and I was detailed this morning to watch you. What do you want from Mr. Stoughton's safe? An honest answer may help you. Nothing else will."

"She was ignorant of his presence"

"I want——" she hesitated, eyeing him over with an insight and an undoubted air of self-command which told the hardy rascal that in this woman he was likely to meet his match. "I want some securities of Mr. Stoughton's which he has ordered me to dispose of for him. I am in his confidence, as I can prove to you if you will give me the opportunity. I have papers at home that will satisfy any one of my right to open this safe and to negotiate such papers as are designated in Mr. Stoughton's cablegrams."

"I don't doubt it." The words came easily from the mobile lips of the wily Beau Johnson. "But it was not to do Mr. Stoughton's business that you opened the safe just now. You have had no orders to-day; you had no order yesterday. Another purpose is in your mind—a personal purpose. It is this abuse of Mr. Stoughton's confidence which brings me here. *You want three thousand dollars badly!*"

 THREE THOUSAND DOLLARS

CHAPTER XIV

"You do not answer"

S HE recoiled. Strong as she was, she was not proof against this surprise.

"How do you know that?" she asked, her voice losing its clear tone. "I do not deny it, but how could you know what I thought to be a secret between—"

"You and your lover? Well—we—the police know many things, young lady. We have a gift. We also have a kind of foreknowledge. I could tell you something of your future if you will deign to listen to me. Your lover is an honest man. What do you suppose he will do when he hears that you have been arrested for attempted burglary on your employer's effects?"

He had been slowly advancing as he reeled off these glib sentences, but he paused as he met her smile. It was not of the same sort as his, but it was not without a certain suggestiveness which he felt it would be best for him to understand before he threw off his mask.

"I don't know what he will do," said she, meeting the false detective's eye as she laid her hand on the safe, "but I know what I shall do if you carry out the purpose you threaten. Show my papers to the police and demand evidence of my having any bad intentions in opening this safe this morning. I think you will have difficulty in producing any. I think that you will only prove yourself a fool. Are you so strong with the authorities as to brave that?"

Astonished at her insight and more than astonished at her self-control, the experienced cracksman paused, and then in tones he rarely used, remarked quietly:

"You are playing with your life, Miss Lee. I have a pistol leveled at you from my pocket, and I'm the man to fire if you give me the slightest occasion to do so. I'm Beau Johnson, miss, a detective if you please, but also a tolerably experienced cracksman, and I want a taste of those bonds."

"And Mr. Fellows?"

The words rang out clear and fearlessly.

"Oh, he? He's a muff. You needn't concern yourself about him. The matter's between us two. Three thousand dollars for you, and a little more, perhaps, for me, and I to take all the blame."

Her eye stole toward the door. No one could enter that way, she knew. Even her screams, if she survived them, might alarm, but could not bring her help for several minutes, if not longer. Yet she did not tremble; only grew a shade paler.

"You do not answer. What have you to say?"

"This." She was like marble now. "You will not kill me, because that would be virtually to kill yourself. You cannot leave this room without my help, nor fire a shot without being caught like a rat in a trap. I want three thousand dollars, and I mean to have them, but I do not see how you are going to get the few more which you promise yourself. Certainly I am not going to aid you in doing so, and you cannot open that safe. You have not the musical training."

"No." The word came like a shot, possibly in lieu of a shot, for if ever he felt murderous it was at that moment. "I have not a musical training, but that does not make me helpless. In a few moments I shall have the pleasure of hearing you test your voice again. There's the office clock ticking; count the strokes."

She stood fascinated. What did he mean by this? Involuntarily she did his bidding.

"One, two, three, four, five, six, seven, eight, nine, ten, *eleven*!"

THREE THOUSAND DOLLARS

"Yes," he repeated, "eleven! And at half past your old father dies."

"Dies?" Her lips did not frame the words; her eyes looked it, her whole sinking, suddenly collapsing figure gave voice to the maddening query, "*Dies?*"

CHAPTER XV

"Now, if Fellows will stay away"

"YES. Such is the understanding if I do not telephone my pals to hold off. He's not at home; he's with my friends. They don't care very much about old men, and if I have not a decent show of money by half-past eleven this morning the orders are to knock him on the head. It won't take a very hard knock. He was far from being in prime condition this morning."

She had shown great feeling at the beginning of this address, but at its close she drew herself up again and met him with something of her old composure.

"These are all lies," said she. "My father would never leave his house at the instigation of any gang. In the first place, he is not strong enough to attempt the stairs. You cannot deceive me in this fashion."

"He might be carried down."

"He wouldn't submit to that, nor would the other lodgers in the house allow it without an express order from me."

"They got the order; not from you, but from him. He demanded to be allowed to go. You see, Mr. Fellows sent a message that you were hurt—I will speak the whole truth, and say dying. The old man could not be held after that. He went with the messenger."

Her cheeks were now like ashes. She had gauged the man before her and felt that he was fully capable of this villainy. How great a villainy she alone knew who had the history of this old man in her heart.

"He went with the messenger," repeated Johnson, watching her face with a cruel leer. "That messenger knew where to take him. You

                                        THREE THOUSAND DOLLARS

may be sure it was to a place quite unknown to the police and to every one else but myself. Five minutes more gone, miss. In just twenty-five minutes more you will be an orphan and one impediment to your marriage will be at an end. How about the other?"

"Oh!" she wailed. "If I could really believe you!"

"I can smooth away that doubt. If you will promise not to compromise me with the clerks or any one inside there, I will allow you to telephone home and learn the truth of what I have told you. Anything further will end all business between us and wind up your father's affairs at the hour set. I can afford to humor you for ten minutes more in this nonsense."

"I will do it," she cried. "I must know what I am fighting before——" She caught herself back, but he was quite able to finish the sentence for her.

"Before you submit to the inevitable," he smiled.

Her head fell and he pointed toward the door.

"I will trust you to guard my—our interests," said he. "Open and go directly to your own telephone."

With a staggering step she obeyed. Creeping up stealthily behind her he watched her manner of opening the door and profited by the one quick glance he got of the office as she stepped through and passed hurriedly forward to her desk. There was no one within sight. Mr. Fellows had not yet returned and the clerks were too remote to notice her agitation or pay attention to her gait or the tremulousness of her tone as she called for her home number.

"Couldn't be better," thought he. "Now if Fellows will stay away long enough, I'll be able to double the boodle I've promised myself." This with a chuckle.

Meantime Miss Lee had got in her message. The answer sent her flying toward him.

"He's gone! He's gone!" she gasped. "My old, old father! Oh, you wretch! Save him and——"

"You save me first," he whispered, and was about to draw her back into the room with the safe, when the outer door opened and a stranger entered on business.

Her agony at the interruption and the few necessary words it involved caused the visitor to stare. But she was able to make herself intelligible and to turn him over to one of the clerks, after which she rejoined Johnson, closing the door quietly behind her.

His greeting was characteristic.

"You waste breath," said he, "by all this emotion. You'll need it to open the safe."

"What guarantee have I that you will keep your part of the contract?" she cried. "I sing—the door opens—you help yourself, and you go. That does not restore to me my father."

"Oh, I'll play fair. In proof of it, here's my pistol. If on our going out I do not stop with you at the telephone and let you communicate with your father and send my own message of release, then shoot me in the back. I give you leave."

Taking the pistol he held out, she cocked it, and looking into the chambers, found they were all full.

"I know how to use it," she said simply.

Admiration showed in his face. He bowed and pointed toward the tube.

"Now for the song," he cried.

CHAPTER XVI

"It was not paper I meant to have"

WITH a bound she took her stand. She was white as death and greatly excited. Watching her curiously, the crafty villain noted the quick throbbing of her throat and the feverish grip on the pistol.

"Time is galloping," he remarked.

She gave a gasp, opened her lips and essayed to sing. An awful, indescribable murmur was all that could be heard. Stiffening herself, she resolutely calmed down her agitation and tried again. The result was but little better than before. Turning with a cry, she looked with horror-stricken eyes into the unmoved, slightly sardonic face of the man behind her.

"I cannot sing! You have frightened away my voice. I cannot raise that note even to save my father's life. I'm choking, choking." Then as she caught the devilish gleam lighting up his eye, she added, "You will never have those thousands! The safe is closed to us both."

He laughed, a very low, cautious laugh, but it made her eyes distend with uncertainty and dread.

"You fail to do justice to my forethought," said he.

"I took this into my calculations. I know women; they can be wicked enough, but they lack coolness. Let me see now what I can do. I cannot sing, but I have a little *aide de camp* which can."

Walking away from her, he approached a small table on which stood an object she had never seen in that room before. It was covered with a cloth, and as he removed this cloth, she reeled with surprise; then she became still with hope and the rush of fresh and overpowering emotions.

A graphophone stood revealed, one of the finest quality. It was set to play the air so often on her lips, and in another moment that keen, high note rang through the room,—that and no more.

It answered. Slowly, softly, after one breathless moment, the door they both watched with fascinated gaze swung slowly ajar, just as they had seen it do at the beginning of this interview, and Johnson, coming forward, pulled it open with a jerk and began to fumble among the contents of the safe.

She could have killed him easily. He had forgotten—but so had she, and there was no one else by to remind her. Had there been, he would have seen a strange spectacle, for no sooner had Johnson's hand struck those shelves and minute drawers, than Grace Lee's whole attitude and expression changed. From a terrified, incapable woman, she became again her old self, strong, self-controlled, watchful. Creeping up behind him, she looked over his shoulders as he examined with his quick, experienced eye the various papers he drew out, noting his anger and growing disappointment as he found them unavailable for immediate use. Conscious of her presence, his rage grew till it shot forth in words. Not stinting oaths, he whirled on her after a moment and asked where the securities were. "*You* meant to have them; you know where the ready money is. Show me, show me at once or——"

Then a great anguish passed across her face, a look of farewell to hopes sweet and dearly cherished. If he saw it he did not heed. All his evil, indomitable will shone in the eye he turned up askance at her, and though she held the means of killing him in her hand, she bowed to that will, and leaning over him, she whispered in his ear:

"It was not paper I meant to have, but—but something else—I——"

She stopped, for breath was leaving her. His slim, assured hand was straying toward a certain knob hidden partly from sight, but plain to the touch if his fingers crept that way.

　　　　　　　　　　　THREE THOUSAND DOLLARS

"Listen!" She was gasping now, but her hand laid on his shoulder emphasized her words. "There are jewels at the other end; Mrs. Stoughton's bridal jewels. They are worth thousands. I—I—meant to take those. They are in a compartment under that lower drawer. Yes, yes—there they are; take them and be gone. I—I have lost—but you will give me back my father? See! there are not many minutes left. Oh, be merciful and——"

CHAPTER XVII

HE was looking at the jewels, appraising them, making sure they were real and marketable. She was looking at them, too, with a wild longing and a bitter disappointment, which he, turning at that moment to mark her looks, saw and rated at its full value.

"Well, I guess they'll do," he exclaimed, pausing in his task of thrusting the gems in his pocket to hand her a bracelet ornamented with one small diamond. "But I expected more from all this fuss and feathers. Was it to guard these——"

"Yes," she murmured, thrusting the bracelet into the neck of her dress and stepping quickly back. "They are priceless to the owner. Associations you know. Mrs. Stoughton is dead—There! that will do. Now for my part of the bargain," and bethinking her at last of the pistol, she raised it and pointed it full in his face. "You will close that door now and send the telephone you promised."

He rose and banged to the door.

"All right," he cried. "You've behaved well. Now hide that pistol in your waist and we'll step into the outer office."

She did as she was bid, and in a moment more they were crossing the floor outside. As they did so, she noticed that the two clerks had been sent out to luncheon, leaving them alone with Mr. Fellows. This was not encouraging, nor did she like the click which at this moment Beau Johnson made with his tongue. It sounded like a preconcerted signal. Whether so or not, it brought Mr. Fellows from his room, and in another instant he was standing with them before the telephone. There was a clock over the safe-room door. It stood at just twenty-five minutes after eleven.

"Hurry!" she whispered as the other took up the receiver.

She did not need to say it. His own anxiety seemed to be as great as hers, but his anxiety was to be gone. The nerve which sustained him while the issue was doubtful gave some slight tokens of failing, now that his efforts had brought success and only this small obligation lay between him and the enjoyment of the booty he had won at such a risk. She was sure that his voice trembled as he uttered the familiar. "Hello!" and during the interchange of words which followed, the strain was perhaps as great on him as on her.

"Hello! how's the old man?"

She could hear the answer. It swept her fears away in a moment.

"Well, but anxious about the girl."

"She's all right, everything's all right. Take the sick man home and tell him that his daughter will be there almost as soon as he is."

"I must hear my father's voice." It was Grace who was speaking. "I will give a cry that will echo through this building if you do not put me in communication with him at once."

Her hand went out to the receiver.

The veins on Beau Johnson's forehead stood out threateningly.

"Curse you!" he muttered; but he gave the order just the same.

"Hello! Don't shut off. The girl's nervous; wants to hear her father's voice. Have him up! two words from him will answer."

"Father!"

Grace's mouth was at the phone.

No reply.

She cast one look at Johnson.

"They're getting him on his feet," he grumbled. *His* eye was on the door.

"Father!" she called again, her voice tremulous with doubt and anxiety.

A murmur this time, but she recognized it.

"It's he! it's he," she cried. "He's safe; he's well. *Father!*"

But Johnson had no time for dilly-dallying. Catching the receiver back, he took his place again at the phone and shouted a few final injunctions. Then he faced her with the question:

"Are you satisfied?" She nodded, speechless at last and almost breathless from exhaustion. He bowed and made for the door. As he opened it, Mr. Fellows slid forward and joined him. Both were leaving. He as well as Johnson. She caught the look which the manager threw her as he closed the door behind them. There was threat in that look and her heart strings tightened as she stood alone there facing her fearful duty. Mr. Fellows was a thief! The manager of this concern was even then perhaps walking off with the booty wrenched from her care by the devil's own inquisition. What should she do? Send for Philip? Yes, that was all her tortured mind could grasp. She would send for her own Philip and get his advice before she notified the police or sent the inevitable cablegram. She was too ill, too shaken to do more. Philip! Philip!

She was fainting—she felt it, and was raising her voice to call in one of the clerks, when the outer door opened and Mr. Fellows came in. She had not expected him back. She had fondly believed that he had gone with his professional comrade; and the sight of him caused her to rise again to her feet.

"You!" she murmured, facing him in dull wonder at his renewed look of threat. "I cannot stay in the same room with you. You are—"

CHAPTER XVIII

"What have you done among you"

"NEVER mind me," came clearly and coldly from his lips. "It is of yourself you must think. Here, officer!" he cried, opening the door again and ushering in a man in plain clothes, but evidently one of the force. "This is the young lady. I accuse her of taking advantage of her power to open Mr. Stoughton's private safe to steal his jewels. Her confederate has escaped. He had a pistol and I had no means of stopping him. But she is right here and you will make no mistake in arresting her. The booty is on her, and smart as she is, she cannot deny that proof."

With a cry, Grace's hand went up to her throat.

Then she settled into her usual self once more.

The officer, eyeing her, asked what she had to say for herself.

"A great deal," was her low answer. "But I shall not say it here. If Mr. Fellows will go with me to wherever you take people suspected of what you suspect me, I can soon make plain my position. But first I should like to send for my friend, Mr. Philip Andrews. He is with the Stickney Company, and he is acquainted with my affairs and the understanding between Mr. Stoughton and myself by which I have access to that gentleman's safe and do much of his private business for him."

"That's all right. Send for Mr. Andrews if you wish, but you mustn't expect to talk to him without witnesses. Is that your coat and hat?"

"Yes."

"Well, put them on."

Mr. Fellows advanced and whispered something in the officer's ear. Immediately the suspicious look grew in his eyes, and he watched her every movement with increased care. She saw this and stepped up to him.

"I shall not deny having this piece of jewelry about my person," she said, drawing the bracelet from its hiding place. "The man whom Mr. Fellows calls my confederate gave it to me and I took it; but it will be hard for him or any one else to prove that it is a theft, harder than it will be for me to prove who is the real culprit here and the man whom you ought to arrest. Watch me, but watch him also; he is more deserving of your close attention than I am."

Her disdain, her poise, the beauty which came out on her face when she was greatly stirred, gave her a striking appearance at that moment. The officer stared, then followed her glance toward Mr. Fellows. What he saw in him made him thoughtful. Turning back to Miss Lee, he said kindly enough, "Will you let me have that bracelet?"

She passed it over and he thrust it in his pocket.

"Now," said he, "I will go first. In a few minutes follow me and go down Nassau Street. A carriage will be at the curb. Take it. As for Mr. Fellows—"

"I cannot leave till some of the clerks come in."

"We will all wait till a clerk comes."

Mr. Fellows paled.

"Here is one now."

The door opened and Philip Andrews came in.

"The door opened and Philip Andrews came in"

"Oh, Philip!"

"What is this? What have you done among you?"

It was no wonder he asked. At sight of him Grace Lee had fainted.

CHAPTER XIX

"So that was your motive"

TWO hours later Grace was explaining herself. She was still pale, but very calm now, though a little sad. The sadness was not occasioned by any doubt she felt about her father. She had telephoned home and learned that he had arrived there and was well, and had nothing but good to say of his captors. No, there was another cause for her manifest depression, a cause not disconnected with Philip, toward whom her eyes ever and anon stole with an uneasy appeal which her mother would have been troubled to see. But it comforted Fellows, who began to regard her threats as idle in face of the evidence of her complicity as afforded by the concealed bracelet.

The officer on duty was questioning her. Had she done this and that? Yes, she had. Why? Then she told her story—the story you have already read. As she proceeded with it, every eye sparkled under the graphic tale, and the police, who had some acquaintance with Beau Johnson, recognized his hand in all that she told. One face only wore a sneer, and that was Fellows's. But no sneer could discredit a story told with such vim and straightforward earnestness. As she mentioned the emptying of the office, each person present turned and gave him a look. The manager had undertaken a piece of work too big for him. His explanations of the presence of the graphophone in this inner office were feeble and contradictory.

But he had his revenge, or thought he had, when she came to the jewels. She had pointed them out, but only to save a worse disaster. Injury to her father? "Yes, and———" She paused and her voice thrilled. "In one of the secret drawers," she continued, "there was an immense amount of currency in large denominations, the loss of which would cripple the business, if not bankrupt Mr. Stoughton. His hand was feeling its way along the face of this drawer. In another moment he would have discovered the tiny knob by the manipulation of which this drawer opens. To save the struggle which would have ensued, I directed his attention elsewhere. I don't believe I did wrong."

"But you accepted one of these articles as your share. Do you believe you did right in this?"

"Yes. I will not mention the smallness of the share, for that makes the portion saved for the owner of little account. Yet that portion is saved. I wish it had been a larger one."

"No doubt. So that was your motive—to save this souvenir for Mr. Stoughton?"

Casting a proud look at Philip, she moved a step nearer to the table on which the bracelet lay. "Will you be good enough," she asked her interrogator, "to take up that bracelet and read the initials on the inner side?"

"R. S. T.," read the official.

"Does any one here know Mrs. Stoughton's maiden name?"

Evidently not, for all remained silent.

"Does any one here know my mother's maiden name?"

Philip started.

"Yes," he cried, "I do. Her name was Rhoda Selden Titus."

"'R. S. T.' read the official"

"R. S. T.," smiled Grace. "This bracelet was my mother's. Mr. Stoughton allowed me to place this keepsake and some other valuables of mine in his private safe. Gentlemen, the whole of those jewels were mine—my sole and only fortune. I was keeping them for"—her eyes stole toward Philip—"for my marriage portion, the secret and great surprise I had planned for my future husband. They are worth some five thousand dollars—my mother was the daughter of a wealthy man. They would have given us a home if I could have kept them; they would also have given my husband a start in business, and this I should have preferred, but I could not let Mr. Stoughton's securities be endangered, and so they had to go. Philip, cannot you forgive me when you think that it was through my folly the secret of the safe became known?"

"I forgive you?" He could not show his feelings, but his eyes were eloquent; so were Fellows's; so were those of the various officials.

"You can prove these statements, Miss Lee?" asked one.

"Easily," she replied.

Then they turned to Fellows.

CHAPTER XX

GRACE never got back her jewels. The wily Johnson was not caught, though Fellows turned state's evidence and did all he could to have the professional netted in the same manner as himself. But she did not suffer from this loss. When Mr. Stoughton learned the full particulars of this daring robbery, he made good to her the value of those jewels, and the prosperity of this young couple was secured. He was even present at the wedding. Grace wore her mother's bracelet, but on her breast was a jewel of far greater value. On its back was engraved,

> To brave G. L.
>
> From her grateful friend, T. S.

"He was even present at the wedding"